The Bears'
COUNTING
Book

Robin and Jocelyn Wild

A Harper Trophy Book

Harper & Row, Publishers

Also by Robin and Jocelyn Wild
The Bears' ABC Book

The Bears' Counting Book
Copyright © 1978 by Robin Wild and Jocelyn Wild
All rights reserved. No part of this book may be used or
reproduced in any manner whatsoever without written permission
except in the case of brief quotations embodied in critical
articles and reviews. Printed in the United States of America.
For information address J. B. Lippincott Junior Books, 10 East 53rd
Street, New York, N.Y. 10022. Published simultaneously in
Canada by Fitzhenry & Whiteside Limited, Toronto.
First American Edition, 1978.
Published in hardcover by J. B. Lippincott, New York.
First Harper Trophy edition, 1985.

Library of Congress Cataloging in Publication Data
Wild, Robin.
  The bears' counting book.

  Summary: Three mischievous bears introduce numbers from one
to ten and twenty to fifty while exploring an empty house.
  [1. Counting books.   2. Bears—Fiction]   I. Wild, Jocelyn,
jt. author.   II. Title.
PZ7-W64576Be   [E]   78-799
ISBN 0-397-31808-1
ISBN 0-06-443074-X (pbk.)

One day three little bears went for a walk.
They found a house.
 "Let's go inside," said Griff.
 "Do you think we should?" asked Snuff.
 "There's no one at home," said Pawpaw.
He pushed open the door and went in.
 All by itself in the hall stood

tick

tick

1
one clock

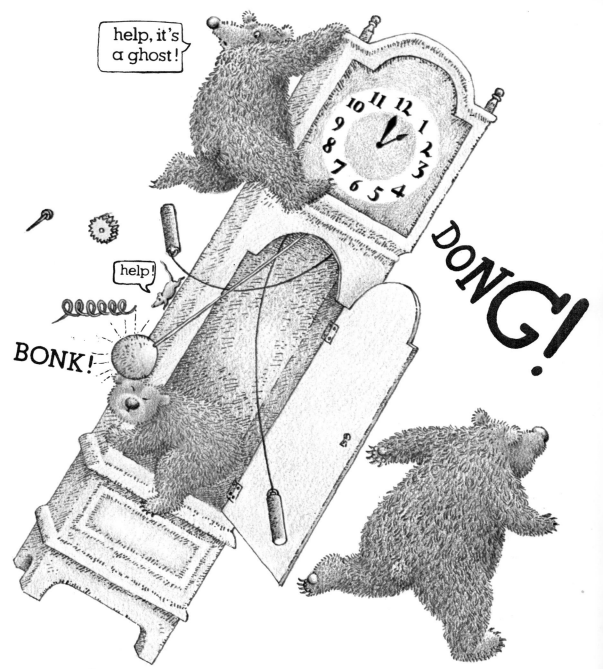

"There's someone inside," whispered Snuff.
"I'll have a look," said Pawpaw. Very
quietly he opened the little door.
All of a sudden the clock struck one.
The bears were so frightened they rushed into
the next room and hid behind

2
two chairs

until it was safe to come out. Griff
climbed into the rocking chair and rocked so
hard that it turned right over.
    "Let's look round," said Snuff.
    The bears ran upstairs. In the bedroom were

3
three beds

The bears bounced on the beds and hit
each other with the pillows.

Suddenly Griff's nose began to twitch.

"I smell something to eat," he said.

He sniffed his way down the stairs and
into the kitchen, where he saw

4

four pans

Three of the pans were empty, but the
fourth was full of oatmeal. Griff gobbled
it all up.

Upstairs in the bedroom, Snuff and Pawpaw
found a chest with

5

five drawers

They pulled out all the drawers and tried on some of the clothes.

In the bottom drawer there were

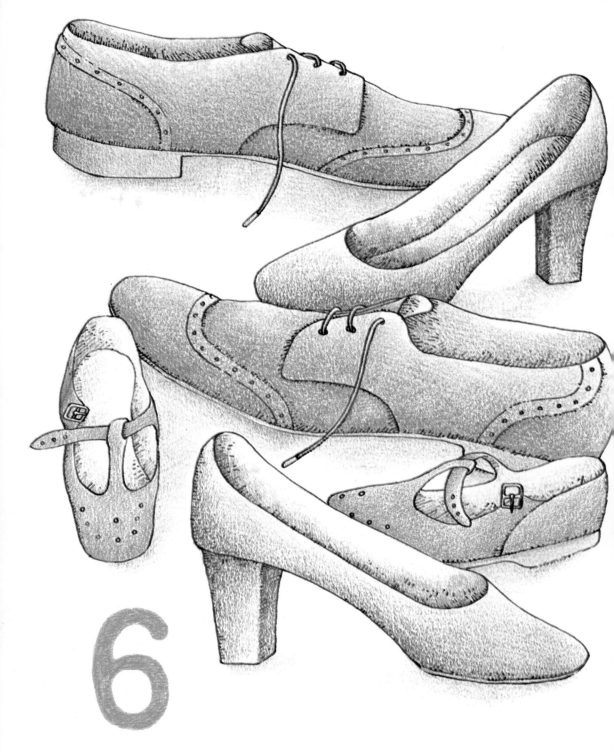

6

six shoes

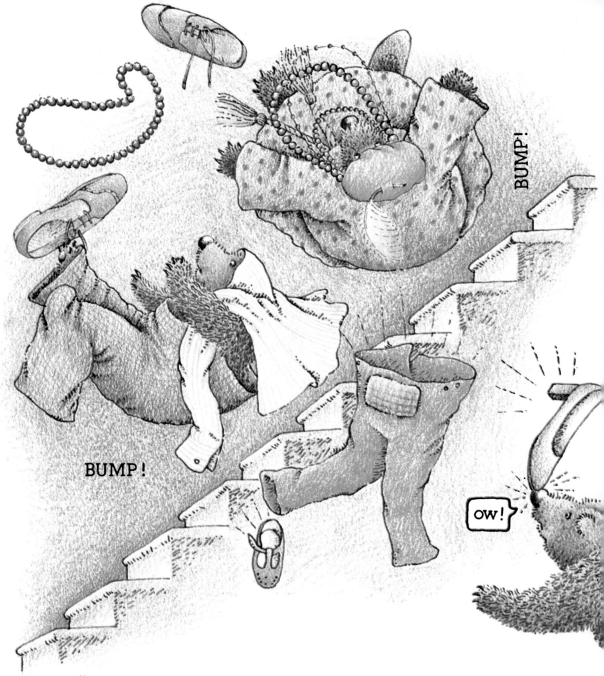

BUMP!

BUMP!

ow!

"You put them on your paws," said Snuff,
"and walk about like this."
But the shoes were too big. Snuff and Pawpaw
fell over and bounced all the way downstairs.
Pawpaw was just starting to cry when Griff
showed him

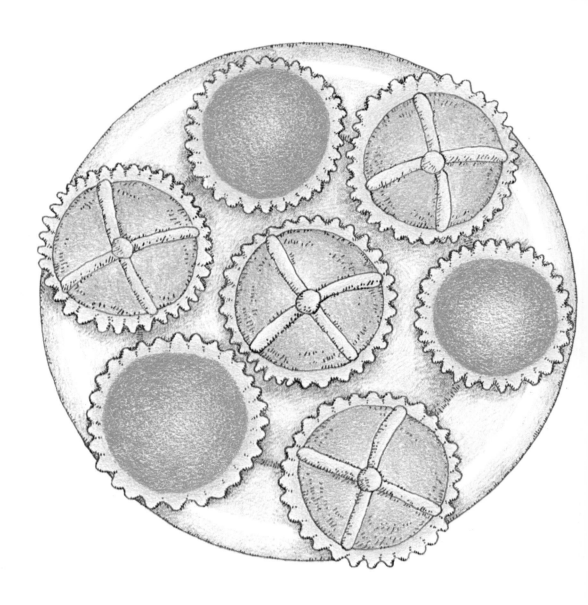

7

seven tarts

CRUNCH!

MUNCH!

"Here you are, Pawpaw," said Griff. "Snuff
and I will have two each and you can have
three because you hurt yourself."
    Soon there was not a crumb left.
    "I'm thirsty," said Snuff. In the
kitchen he found

8

eight bottles

"I'm having this yellow one," said Griff,
and he took a big gulp of mustard sauce.
  "Help, I'm on fire!" he spluttered.
  "We'll cool you down," said Snuff and Pawpaw.
They poured milk all over Griff, and he soon
felt better. He climbed up to some shelves with

9

nine plates

"I wonder what's in that pot up there,"
said Griff. He reached for the pot and three
plates fell off and smashed.
   The bears hurried away into another room.
On the floor were

10

ten toys

BROOM!
BROOM!

WHOOPS!

"Quick march!" shouted Snuff. But clumsy
Griff tripped, and they all fell down.

"I've had enough of this game," said Pawpaw,
"I want to see what's in the garden."

By the back door was a little shed. The
bears peered inside and saw

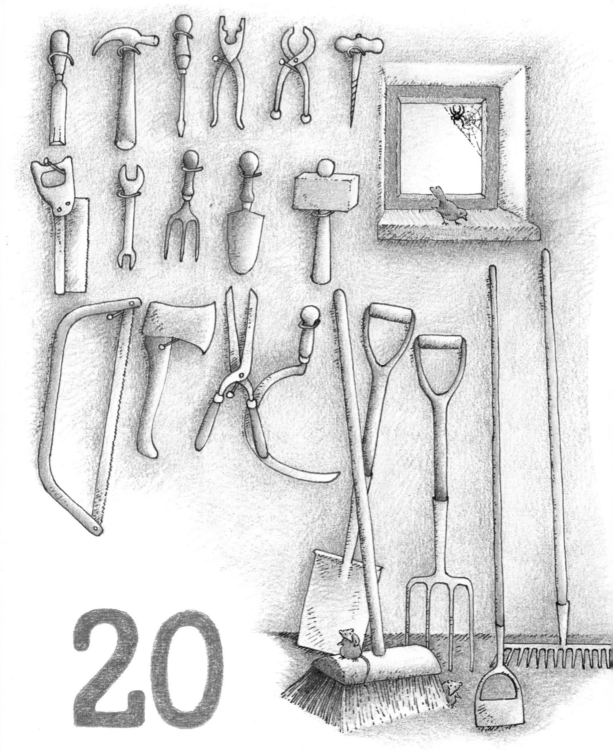

20
twenty tools

"I'm digging a tunnel with this shovel,"
said Griff.

"We're going exploring," called Snuff
and Pawpaw, and off they went.

In a corner of the garden stood a hen
house. Pawpaw undid the door. Out fluttered

30

thirty hens

"You can have a little walk, hens, and
then you must go back in," said Pawpaw.
    But when the bears tried to chase the hens
back inside, they just ran about clucking.
    Snuff and Pawpaw left the hens and went
off to watch Griff feeding cabbages to

40

forty cows

"Oh dear," said Pawpaw, "those cows are
very big. We'd be much safer if we climbed
up that apple tree."

In the tree Pawpaw counted

fifty apples

Those bears ate apples until they were
so full they fell fast asleep under the tree.
   After a while a car drove up. It was
the family who lived in the house.
   The bears woke with a fright and ran off
as fast as they could back home to the woods.

What a mess the family found in their house!
Griff, Snuff and Pawpaw began to feel sorry
for the naughty things they had done. Early
next morning they came back to the house.
And when the little boy opened the front door
he had a surprise; for there on the step lay a
pile of mushrooms, a bunch of flowers and a
great big sticky chunk of honeycomb.